THE WONDERFUL BOX

THE
WONDERFUL BOX

by Mildred Ames

illustrated by Richard Cuffari

E. P. Dutton　　　New York

Text copyright © 1978 by Mildred Ames
Illustrations copyright © 1978 by Richard Cuffari

Library of Congress Cataloging in Publication Data

Ames, Mildred.   The wonderful box.

SUMMARY: Three children find a large, beautifully-
wrapped box, turn it in at the police station, and wait
thirty days wondering what is inside.

I. Cuffari, Richard, date   II. Title.
PZ7.A5143Wo   [E]   77-5628   ISBN 0-525-43200-0

Published in the United States by E. P. Dutton, a Division
of Sequoia-Elsevier Publishing Company, Inc., New York
Published simultaneously in Canada by Clarke,
Irwin & Company Limited, Toronto and Vancouver

Editor: Ann Durell

Printed in the U.S.A.   First Edition
10 9 8 7 6 5 4 3 2 1

to Alida

It was while Mama was at work that Grover, Midge, and Joey found the wonderful box. That day Grover stood for a long time on the front porch. He watched his friend Buzzy pedal a new bike up and down the street. No hands.

The big show-off, Grover thought. All the same, Grover wished *he* had a bicycle. Even Buzzy's old one. Then he could get a paper route. With a paper route, he could earn money to help Mama.

Grover's younger sister, Midge, sat on the porch steps. She never even saw Buzzy's new bicycle. She was watching the three Lee girls next door as they played hopscotch. None of the girls ever asked Midge to play with them. And Midge was too shy to ask.

I wish I had a friend, Midge thought. Someone to play with.

As Grover watched the bicycle and Midge watched the girls, their little brother, Joey, came home from school. He handed Midge a note.

"It's for Mama," Joey said. "From my teacher. What does it say, Midge?"

Midge read the note. "It says you're still having trouble learning to read."

Joey said, "Mama will really be mad."

"Not mad, Joey—sad."

It seemed to Joey that he always made Mama either mad or sad. Never happy. "Well, I can't help it," he said. "Besides, there's a good reason why I can't read."

"What's that?" Midge asked.

"I can't read because—because—" Joey thought long and hard. Finally he had it. "Because I don't like the letters in books. I just like the pictures."

"That's dumb, Joey," Midge said. "Everybody knows letters spell words. And words spell pictures."

Joey said stubbornly, "Then I wish pictures would spell words. If I had books with pictures that spelled words, I could read."

That afternoon, in an alley near their house, Grover, Midge, and Joey found the box. A box as big as a doghouse. And wrapped like a present with shiny paper and ribbons.

"It must have fallen off a delivery truck," Grover said.

Grover, Midge, and Joey stared at the box. They walked all around it. They touched it.

It was a long time before they decided what to do with it.

Because it was heavy, they put it on Joey's wagon and pulled it around the block to the police station. The officer at the desk said, "We'll keep the box for thirty days. If no one calls for it by then, it will be yours."

On the way home, Joey said, "I wonder what's in the box."

Surely something I could really use, Grover thought.

Surely something I could really have fun with, Midge thought.

Joey thought, Something that would make Mama happy, I bet.

Then they all took guesses, each new guess more wonderful than the last. Was it a doll? A football? A popcorn machine? A million jelly beans? A television set? Even an airplane!

No. It was none of those, Grover was sure. He believed he knew what the box really held. So did Midge. So did Joey. But none of them said a word. For they had all wished on birthday cakes. They knew if you told a wish, it would never come true.

That night they told Mama about the box. The next day Mama told one of the neighbors. Soon everyone on the street knew. And in no time at all, everyone in the neighborhood knew.

When Buzzy heard about the box, he came to see Grover. "I bet there's a tank full of man-eating fish in the box," Buzzy said.

Grover shook his head. "I think I know what's in the box," he said, because he truly believed he did, "but I can't tell."

"I'd be able to guess if I could see the box," Buzzy said. "Would you ask the officer to show it to me?"

"I sure hate to bother him," Grover said. Then he added generously, "I'll soon be part owner of the box. I'll show it to you then."

Buzzy said, "I'd pay a lot to see it now. Even a quarter."

"That's too much," Grover said. But because he had a good head for business, he added, "A nickel would be a fair price. For a nickel I'll ask the officer to show you the box."

Buzzy gave Grover a nickel and they both went to the police station. After the officer gave permission, Grover showed Buzzy the box. When they left, Buzzy was sure he knew what the box held. For he had a wish too.

Buzzy told some kids in school about the wonderful box. And they told their friends. The officer shook his head at the number of boys and girls that walked quietly in and out of the station. All of them said one look at the box was worth every penny of the nickel Grover collected outside the door.

Every day, while Grover collected nickels at the station, Midge sat alone on the front steps.

One afternoon Rosie Lee came over to Midge. "I heard you found a big box," she said.

Midge was too shy to speak. She hung her head.

"Well, if you don't want to tell me about it, you don't have to!" Rosie said in a huff and started to hurry off.

Midge thought of the wonderful box and of how much she wanted to tell someone about it.

She took a deep breath and said, "There's a lot to tell."

"Then tell me a lot. If you don't finish today, you can go on tomorrow. And the day after, too."

So every day Midge told Rosie about the box. And every day there seemed more to say. And every day Rosie made a game of guessing all the wonderful gifts the box might hold. An Arabian horse? Too big? A Shetland pony then. It was easy for Rosie to make jokes about it, for she had never seen the box.

While Grover collected nickels and while Midge told Rosie about the box, Joey too was busy. One afternoon he went to the police station. "Did you find out what's in the box?" he asked the policeman.

The officer had children of his own, so he knew something about wishes. Although he was tired of all the boys and girls coming in and out of the station, he spoke kindly to Joey.

"No, I haven't found out what's in the box. There's a card with it, though. Maybe that will tell."

Joey had to climb up on a chair to reach the box. He found a small envelope hidden under the big satin bow. The card inside the envelope had letters on it that looked like chicken scratchings to Joey.

Although Joey was bad at letters, he was good at numbers. So he counted the letters and went home.

The next day he said to his teacher, "There
are ten letters I want to know."

His teacher said, "I can't possibly guess which
ten letters you mean, Joey, so you'll simply have
to learn all twenty-six. But I've never been able
to teach you even one."

"Then I'll just have to teach myself," Joey said.

For thirty days the wonderful box sat on a
table at the police station. Grover collected
nickels for a look at it. Midge told Rosie all about
it. And Joey learned twenty-six letters to find
out what was inside it.

When the thirty days were up, Grover, Midge, and Joey went to the station. Buzzy went along too. So did Rosie. But when they got there, the wonderful box was gone!

"I'm sorry," the officer said. "The owner came for the box about an hour ago."

Stunned, Grover, Midge, and Joey looked at each other. Then they all stared at the table where, only yesterday, the wonderful box had sat. Nothing but the small envelope remained. They felt sick with disappointment.

The officer said, "The owner left a reward for you in the envelope."

Joey climbed up on a chair to reach it. He took out money and, because he was good at numbers, divided the reward three ways. They all walked quietly and sadly home together.

Then Grover thought about the bicycle he had wanted. He jangled the nickels in his pocket. He felt the reward money. It gave him an idea. He said to Buzzy, "Hey—how about selling me your old bicycle?"

Buzzy agreed right away because he had wished very hard for someone to race him.

In front of her house, Midge said to Rosie, "There isn't any box to talk about now. I guess I'll have to go sit on the front steps by myself again."

"Who needs to talk about some silly old box?" Rosie said, because she had never seen the box. "Come and play hopscotch with me. I'm tired of playing with my sisters. I'd rather play with a friend."

Midge smiled happily. "First, let's go to the drugstore with my reward money. They make a giant banana split for two friends to share."

Joey still held on to the card from the box. "I'm glad Grover will have a bike," he said. "And I'm glad Midge will get to eat a giant banana split with Rosie. But I'm sorry we'll never know what was in the box."

Rosie said, "Maybe it tells on the card, Joey."

Joey opened the card. He was surprised to find that the twenty-six letters he had learned jumped around in his head until they spelled pictures. Which was every bit as good as pictures that spelled words.

Joey said, "Now I'll be able to read lots of words." Best of all, he could read the two words on the card.

When he read them to the others, Grover patted the pocket that held money to buy Buzzy's old bicycle and said, "I knew there was something in the box that I could really use."

Midge smiled at her friend Rosie and said, "I knew there was something in the box that I could really have fun with."

Joey looked at the words he could read and said, "I knew there was something in the box that would make Mama happy."

Buzzy winked at Grover and said, "The box held just what I thought it did."

And it did.

The wonderful box held a wish for every child who saw it. Perhaps all of their wishes came true. But no one will ever know. For everyone agrees, you must never tell wishes. Even when they come true. And especially if, as Joey read, they are—

BEST WISHES

MILDRED AMES writes for children because she shares so many of their beliefs. "Like children, I believe there *can* be happy endings; that people *can* live happily ever after; and that if you wish hard enough and work hard enough, a dream can come true." Referring to *The Wonderful Box,* she adds, "Sometimes you can even find a miracle in the streets." Mrs. Ames lives in Palos Verdes Estates, California.

RICHARD CUFFARI's illustrations for *The Wonderful Box* reflect a part of his daily life. The house and neighborhood in which Grover, Midge, and Joey live are much like his own, in Brooklyn, New York. And the children bear a close resemblance to his young neighbors. Mr. Cuffari, who has illustrated more than 150 books, teaches book illustration at Parsons School of Design in New York City.

The text was set in Caledonia Linotype. The display types are Hydro Outline and Palatino. The halftone art was prepared in pen and ink with wash. Both the art and the book were printed by Halliday Lithographers.

E
A

The Wonderful Box